Deep
in the forest, lived
manybiganimals—
the lion, the elephant, the tiger, the wolf,
the leopard, the fox and some snakes.

They were all good friends and used to meet everyday at the river bank to talk, laugh and play.

The leopard was very proud of the beautiful spots on his body. One day as all the animals got together at the river bank, he

said, "Friends, I have something
to ask you."

All the animals stopped playing and looked at the leopard. "My friends", said the leopard, "I have always wondered why you all consider the lion as the king of the jungle. Am i not better looking than the lion? Look at my beautiful spots!"

Saying this, the leopard turned, first to the left, then to the right, so that all the animals could admire him.

On seeing the vanity of the leopard ,the fox got very angry. He waited for some other

animals to say something, but, they were all too scared .So he decided to talk to the leopard.

"You are very foolish" ,the fox told the leopard. "You are looking just at your outward beauty. It is more important to have a bright brain and a pure heart than to have just a beautiful body."

On hearing the fox speak these wise words, all the other animals began to clap loudly. "We agree with you", they told the fox." Long live our King, the Lion!"

The leopard realised his mistake and walked away, with his tail between his legs, hanging his head in shame.